ISBN 978-1-78270-517-8

This edition first published 2022

Published by Award Publications Limited,
The Old Riding School, Welbeck, Worksop, S80 3LR

 /awardpublications @award.books @award_books
www.awardpublications.co.uk

22-1035 1

Printed in China

The Three Little Kittens

Retold by Sophie Giles

Illustrated by Lesley Smith

award

Once upon a time, there were three little kittens, Daisy, Maisy and Bo. They lived with their mother in a house on top of a hill. One day, there was a knock at the door.

The postman gave them a package. It was from their grandmother. Inside it were three new coats! The three kittens put them on and fastened them up.

"Don't we look smart?" they cried.

"Yes, indeed," said their mother. "I'll knit you all some mittens to wear with your new coats."

She knitted for hours and hours until the mittens were finished. The three little kittens were very happy with their new outfits.

"Take care of your mittens," said their mother. "Mind that you don't lose them."

It was autumn and the days were chilly. The three little kittens wore their mittens every time they left the house to play in the fallen leaves, climb trees and explore. They listened to their mother and took great care of their mittens.

Until one day, when they ran to their mother with tears in their eyes.

"Mama, we're so sorry! We've lost our mittens," they sobbed.

Their mother was busy making a delicious blackberry pie. She turned to look at her three kittens. "You've lost your mittens? You naughty kittens!" she scolded. "Then you shall have no pie."

The three little kittens wiped their eyes and went to look for their mittens.

First, they went to the chicken coop, where a big brown hen was sitting on her eggs.

Knock knock knock.

"Have you seen our mittens, Clucky Hen?" they asked.

"I have not seen your mittens. Have you looked in your pockets?" said Clucky Hen.

The three little kittens emptied their pockets and shook their heads, sadly. They found all sorts of things, but no mittens.

Next, the three little kittens searched their bedroom. They looked in drawers and under the bed, in the wardrobe and on the shelves.

"No mittens there!"

Then they climbed up into the attic to look.

They found was a chest full of old clothes and spent hours dressing up and playing with forgotten toys. But they didn't find their missing mittens.

"We must find our mittens. Where else have we been?" asked Daisy.

"I know!" said Maisy. "We went to pick blackberries."

"And you hurt your thumb on the thorns!" said Bo.

"The blackberry bushes!" the three little kittens miaowed together.

They hurried to the wood. There, they found their mittens hanging from the blackberry bushes, right where they had left them.

The three little kittens put them on and ran home to show their mother.

"You found your mittens, you wonderful kittens," she smiled. "You shall have some pie."

The three little kittens were very hungry. They tucked into the delicious, juicy pie without a second thought. Then...

"Oh no!" they cried. "Look at our mittens!"

The three little kittens ran to show their
mother their messy, sticky mittens.

"You silly kittens," she said. "Sticky thumbs and fingers, messy paws and whiskers! You must wash your mittens and hang them out to dry."

So they filled a bucket with warm water and washing powder. In went their messy mittens and — *swish, bubble, swash* — the three little kittens washed their mittens.

When all of the blackberry juice was washed away,
the three little kittens hung their clean, wet mittens
on the clothes line to dry. Each soggy mitten was
fastened in place with a wooden peg.

When the mittens were dry, the three little kittens
went to show their mother. "Look, Mama! Our mittens
are soft and clean."

"Such clean mittens and such clever kittens. What a very busy day you have had!" said their mother, and she smiled.

Yawning, the three little kittens climbed into their cosy bed. Their mother listened to their soft little snores as they fell fast asleep, dreaming of blackberry pie.

The Three Little Kittens

Three little kittens, they lost their mittens,
And they began to cry,
Oh, Mother dear, we sadly fear
That we have lost our mittens.
What! Lost your mittens, you naughty kittens!
Then you shall have no pie!
Miaow, miaow, miaow,
No, you shall have no pie!

The three little kittens, they found their mittens,
And they began to cry,
Oh, Mother dear, see here, see here,
For we have found our mittens.
Put on your mittens, you silly kittens,
And you shall have some pie.
Purr, purr, purr,
Oh, let us have some pie.

Are you a Ready steady Readers SUPERSTAR?

k n

b t

Silent letters

Race to point to the words in the story that have these silent letters.

OR

Whisper the words that use these silent letters as you read the story aloud.

Different voices

Think about how you could use different voices to show how the characters feel.

Don't we look smart!

We've lost our mittens!

You silly kittens!

Look, find, count and talk!

Can you **find** this crown somewhere in the pictures?

How many pegs did the kittens use to hang their mittens up to dry?

Why do you think the kittens took off their mittens when they were picking blackberries?

Where did the three little kittens search for their lost mittens?

This story is based on a nursery rhyme (see pages 26–27).

Make up your own story about the three little kittens and their mittens. What will happen in your story?

Notes for Grown-Ups

Ready Steady Readers build young readers' vocabulary, develop their comprehension skills and boost their progress towards independent reading.

Research carried out by BookTrust has found that children who are regularly read to, or with, have stronger bonds with their family members, a more positive sense of self, greater well-being and improved educational outcomes, health and creativity.

★ Make storytime fun to grow a love of reading. Build it into your regular routine, whether you're reading aloud, listening to your child read, or reading separate books together. Why not create a special reading space? It could be as elaborate as a decorated den, or as simple as a special cushion on the floor.

★ Be a Reading Role Model: if your child sees you read, they will copy. So let them 'catch' you reading and enjoying a range of books and magazines. Reading opportunities are everywhere, and the key is enjoyment.

★ Encourage your child to read aloud to help pick up and resolve any difficulties they might have. As their skills grow, it will also help their fluency and expression. For older children, 'reading in their head' is an important skill to learn, though reading aloud regularly will help to develop their overall confidence.

★ Work through the activities at the back of the book with your child to help them develop their observation, comprehension and communication skills.

★ Always keep a positive attitude and focus on your child's achievements. You could say, "You found that word tricky, but you kept trying! Well done!" This will boost their confidence and grow their enjoyment of reading.